The Nutcracker

This book belongs to:

_____

_____

This edition published by Parragon Books Ltd in 2016

Parragon Books Ltd
Chartist House
15–17 Trim Street
Bath BA1 1HA, UK
www.parragon.com

Retold by Rachel Elliot
Illustrated by Valeria Docampo
Designed by Kathryn Davies and Anna Madin

ISBN 978-1-4748-3329-5

Printed in China

The Nutcracker

From the story by E. T. A. Hoffmann

PaRragon

Bath • New York • Cologne • Melbourne • Delhi
Hong Kong • Shenzhen • Singapore

It was Christmas Eve and the snow was gently falling. Clara and her brother Fritz were very excited. That night there would be a magnificent party with music and dancing, as well as lots of fantastic presents!

Fritz was busy with his toy soldiers, lining them up and giving them their orders.

Clara put the finishing touches to their enormous tree. She hung shining baubles and candy canes tied with bows from the branches.

"This is my favourite part," Clara said to her brother as she lifted up a beautiful fairy with delicate wings and a sugarplum-coloured dress.

At last, it was time for
the party to begin.

"The guests are arriving!"
cried Clara, peeping out of her
bedroom window.

Fritz came running over to see
who was crunching through the snow.

"Can you see Godfather
Drosselmeyer?" asked Clara.

"Yes, there he is waving!"
cried Fritz. "Come on!"

Their godfather was a famous
toymaker. He made the most magical
toys in the whole city. Clara and Fritz
could hardly wait to see what he had
brought for them.

Godfather Drosselmeyer hugged the children at the door, and with a flourish, he produced two gifts.

Fritz eagerly unwrapped a mechanical gobstopper machine. For Clara, there was a wooden nutcracker in the shape of a soldier.

"Take good care of him," said Godfather Drosselmeyer. "He is very special."

"I love him," Clara whispered. "Thank you."

"But he's a soldier," said Fritz. "He should be mine."

"You can't have him!" cried Clara.

Fritz tried to snatch the Nutcracker away
from her. He pulled and Clara tugged, and then...

CRACK!

The Nutcracker's leg snapped off!

Clara cradled the Nutcracker in her arms and wept.

"Don't cry, Clara," said her godfather gently. "This soldier has been wounded, but I can soon fix him."

Godfather Drosselmeyer pulled a little tool pouch from his pocket and quickly mended the Nutcracker so that he looked as good as new.

"Oh, thank you," said Clara, drying her eyes. "I'll never let anyone hurt him again."

Everyone was dancing now and the house was filled with music and laughter. Clara placed the Nutcracker carefully under the Christmas tree and went to join the party.

Finally, the last dance was danced and the guests said their goodbyes. The family went to bed and the house was dark and quiet.

Bong!

Clara awoke to hear the last bong of the clock striking midnight.

"Oh no!" she thought. "I left the Nutcracker all alone under the tree."

Clara tiptoed downstairs and crept under the Christmas tree, holding the Nutcracker protectively.

Suddenly, the tree started to grow. Taller and taller! Or was it just that Clara was shrinking?

"What's happening?" she cried.

"Don't be afraid," said a kind voice suddenly.
Clara turned around. Her Nutcracker had come alive!
Behind him, Fritz's soldiers were sitting up in their
toy box and Clara's dolls were gazing around.

Before Clara could speak, she heard a scurrying
sound and from every nook and cranny, an army of
mice poured into the room! They were led by
a giant Mouse King with a golden crown.

"ATTACK!" he squealed.

"Who will fight with me?" cried the Nutcracker.
The soldiers marched boldly out of the toy box.

"TO BATTLE!" ordered the Nutcracker.
The soldiers shouted and cheered and the
mice squealed and squeaked.

Suddenly, Clara saw the Mouse King spring
towards her beloved Nutcracker, baring his teeth.
"No!" cried Clara. She snatched off her slipper
and hurled it at the Mouse King. He fell to the ground
with a cry, and his crown tumbled from his head.

With their leader defeated, the mice
scurried away in fear. The battle was won!

The Nutcracker picked up Clara's
slipper and placed it on her foot. She
gasped – the Nutcracker had been
transformed into a handsome prince!

"I owe you my life, Princess Clara," he said.
"You broke the spell that was put on me long
ago by a wicked Mouse Queen."

"I'm glad that you're safe," said Clara.
"But you are mistaken – I'm not a princess."

"Are you sure?" asked the prince.

Clara looked down and saw that she was
wearing a glittering gown and satin shoes!

"Come," said the prince. "I am going to
take you on a wonderful adventure."

The walls of the sitting room seemed to fade away,
and a beautiful sleigh drew up in front of them, led by
two reindeer.

Clara and the prince climbed aboard and they were
swept high into the sky among the sparkling stars.

Suddenly Clara caught sight of a magical land down below. Lollipop trees shimmered on candyfloss hills. There were gingerbread houses and rivers of honey, and an orange-scented breeze.

"Where are we?" gasped Clara.

"This is the Kingdom of Sweets," said the prince.

The sleigh landed beside a rose-coloured lake and changed
into a sea-chariot pulled by dolphins. Swans swam beside them,
and shimmering fish leapt out of the water.

On the far side of the lake was a magnificent marzipan palace. A fairy with delicate wings was waving to them from the gate.

"Look," said the prince. "It's the Sugarplum Fairy!"

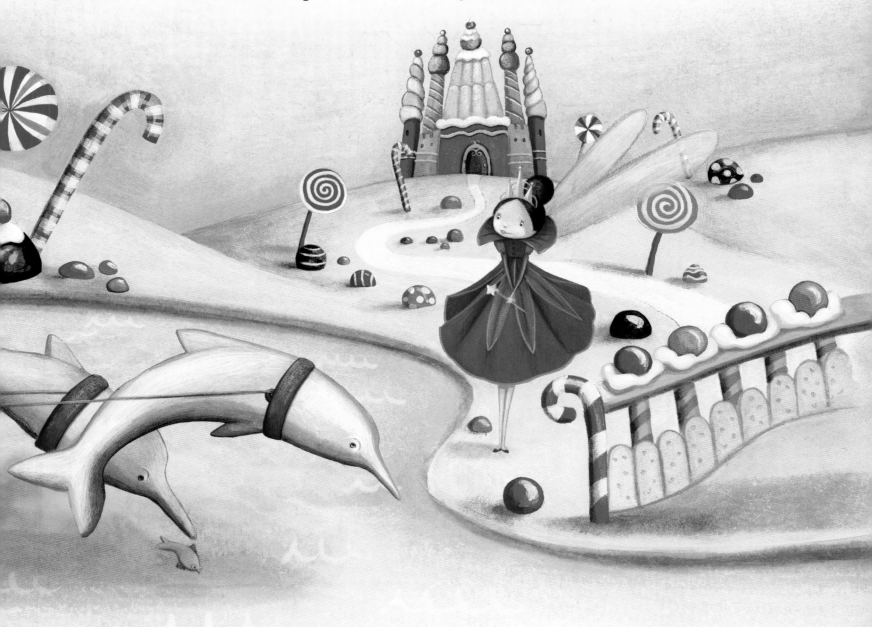

"Prince Nutcracker!" cried the fairy. "You are home at last."

"This is Princess Clara," said the prince, as they stepped ashore. "She saved my life and broke the Mouse Queen's spell."

The Sugarplum Fairy hugged Clara.

"Come and join the celebrations!" she said.

Inside the palace, Clara and the prince
feasted on delicious cakes and sweets.

They watched in wonder as dancers
from every corner of the world whirled
around the room.

Then it was the Sugarplum Fairy's turn. Clara had never seen such dancing! She twirled and twirled until all Clara could see was the blur of her plum-coloured dress.

Clara's eyelids began to droop. Her adventures had made her tired. The sound of the music became fainter and fainter....

When Clara woke up on Christmas morning, she found herself curled up under the Christmas tree next to the Nutcracker. Toys were strewn across the floor and her parents were standing over her.

"What have you been doing?" asked her father.

"Oh, I've had the most wonderful adventure," said Clara.

She told her parents all about the Mouse King, the Nutcracker Prince and the Kingdom of Sweets.

"It was just a dream, darling," said her mother.

Clara gazed up at the sugarplum-coloured fairy on top of the tree. Then she looked at the wooden Nutcracker in her hands.

"Perhaps it was," she said.

Suddenly, Clara noticed something glinting on the carpet and a smile spread across her face. It was a tiny golden crown!

"Merry Christmas, Prince Nutcracker," she whispered.